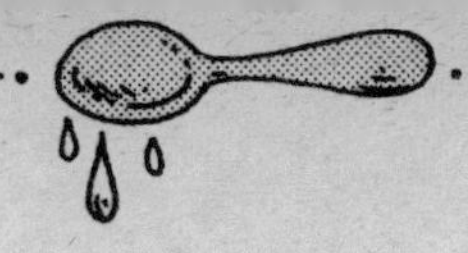

Hey, Gang!
Here's a sample letter from
DON'T STAND IN THE SOUP

Dear Jovial Bob:

Pardon me for asking this, but isn't it true that no one cares if you're rude or polite today? Isn't it true that all the rules of etiquette just don't count anymore?

Phoebe
Des Moines, Iowa

Well . . . yes and no.

When you're at the dinner table, it isn't *really* necessary to know which is the proper fork to use to scratch your nose. But wouldn't you feel more comfortable if you used the same fork everyone else uses?

Good manners make it easier to get along with people. Knowing the right thing to do can make you feel a lot more comfortable.

Which is the proper hand to sneeze in? Which sleeve do you use to remove gravy from your chin at a formal dinner party? What is the polite thing to say to someone after you have roller-skated over his face?

These are all questions that I hope to deal with or ignore completely in this book.

Jovial BoB Stine

Bantam Skylark Books of Related Interest
Ask your bookseller for the books you have missed

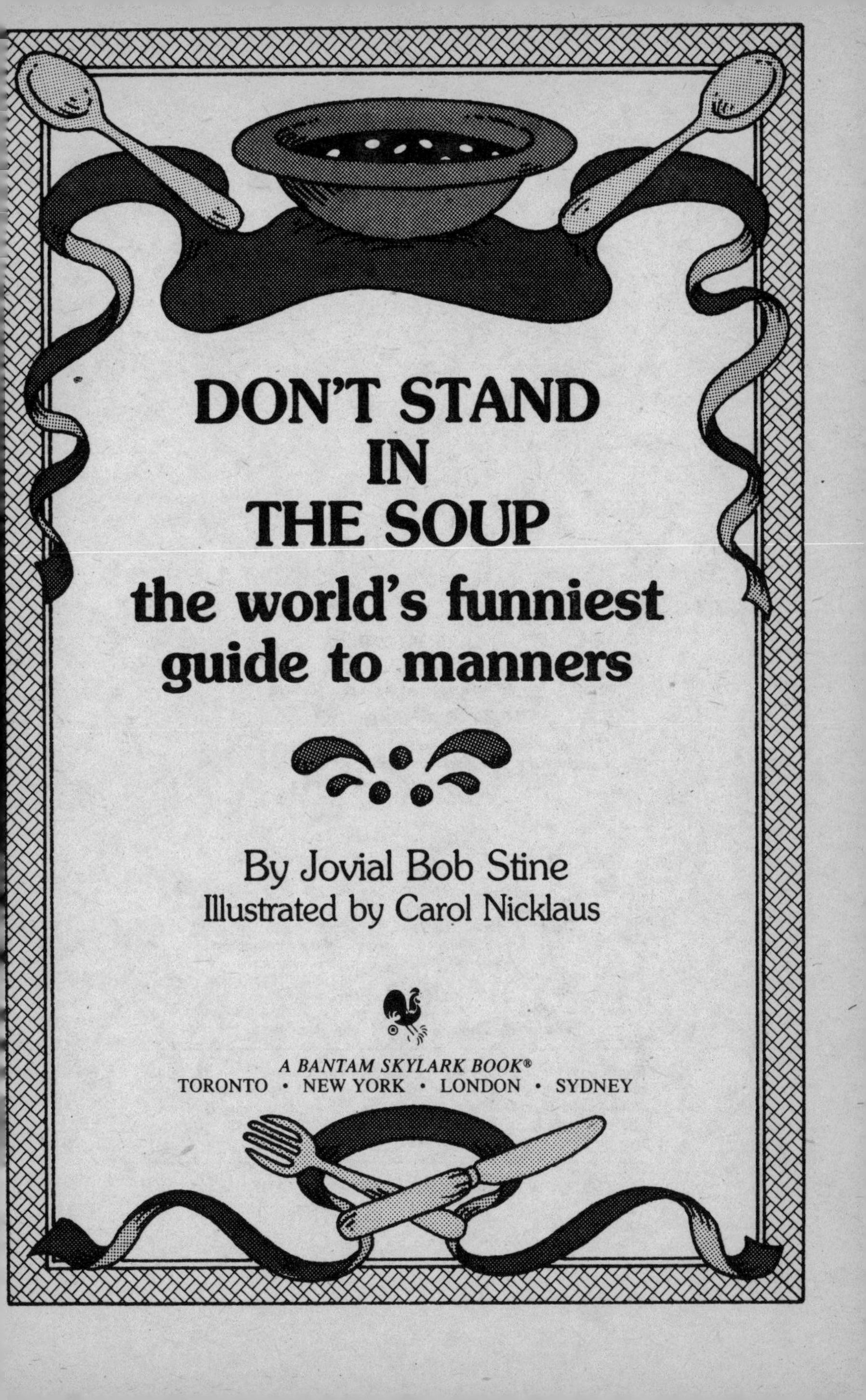

DON'T STAND IN THE SOUP

the world's funniest guide to manners

By Jovial Bob Stine

Illustrated by Carol Nicklaus

A BANTAM SKYLARK BOOK®

TORONTO · NEW YORK · LONDON · SYDNEY

RL 6,009-013

DON'T STAND IN THE SOUP
THE WORLD'S FUNNIEST GUIDE TO MANNERS

A Bantam Skylark Book / April 1982

Skylark Books is a registered trademark of Bantam Books, Inc., Registered in U.S. Patent and Trademark Office and elsewhere.

ISBN 0-553-15096-0

Published simultaneously in the United States and Canada

Bantam Books are published by Bantam Books, Inc. Its trademark consisting of the words "Bantam Books" and the portrayal of a Rooster, is registered in U.S. Patent and Trademark Office and in other countries. Marca Registrada. Bantam Books, Inc., 666 Fifth Avenue, New York, New York 10103.

PRINTED IN THE UNITED STATES OF AMERICA

0 9 8 7 6 5 4 3 2

For Megan
who couldn't be more polite
—Jovial Bob Stine

A special thanks to
Phoebe from Des Moines
—The Editor

contents

introduction

• three introductory letters •

Dear Jovial Bob:
I've never written to you before, but I was just wondering if you are ready to begin answering questions in your book.

Just Wondering
Cleveland, Ohio

Yes, I am ready to begin. Thank you for getting this book off to such a rousing start.

• • • • •

Dear Jovial Bob:

I just finished reading the first letter in your book, and I enjoyed it very much. I also liked the simple, direct way you answered it.

Do you plan to answer all the letters in your book in such a simple, direct way?

Also Wondering
San Diego, California

Yes, I do. That is, I certainly hope to. I mean, I'll try my best. That's kind of my plan. At least, I hope I can.

• • • • •

Dear Jovial Bob:

I loved the first letter in your book, but I was a little disappointed with the second. I'm just wondering how to find things in your book. Is there a system or a plan?

Can you tell us how to find things in the book?

Hopeful
Provo, Utah

I'll be glad to help you find anything. Please call me at home, ask me what you are looking for, and I'll tell you what page it's on. If I'm not at home, leave your name and address and I'll be over for dinner at six p.m. sharp. Please tell your parents not to fuss. I eat most anything—and everything.

Murrrrgle Murrrrgle
BLEMP GLORF

chapter one

introductions and shaking hands

• introductions •

Introducing people to other people is a custom that goes all the way back to 1967. I myself used to worry about having to make introductions until a friend taught me a little trick.

She told me to memorize these letters: BLEMPGLORF. And she said to think of those letters each time I had to introduce someone to someone else.

Believe it or not, this trick works every time. I haven't the foggiest idea what BLEMPGLORF stands for, but I've been less nervous ever since. (Luckily, a lot of my friends are named Blempglorf.)

• • • • •

Dear Jovial Bob:

Introductions must seem easy to adults who have been making them for years. But they can be quite a problem to us younger people. Any suggestions?

Blempglorf
Reno, Nevada

Yes. Introductions can be easy if you follow these three rules:

1. Never introduce a friend to someone who's in the middle of open heart surgery.

2. Never introduce a friend who wears a live bear on his head to your mother.

3. Never memorize rules about making introductions when common sense will do just as well.

• • • • •

Dear Jovial Bob:

I'd like to introduce my boyfriend to my parents, but he refuses to get out of his car. What should I do?

Puzzled
Dallas, Texas

Tell him to make a right turn in the dining room and park in front of the couch. Remember when you're making the introduction that it isn't necessary for your boyfriend to stand—unless he's driving a convertible.

• • • • •

Dear Jovial Bob:

Are there any special rules for introducing a shorter person to a taller person?

Phoebe
Des Moines, Iowa

Yes. When introducing a shorter person to a taller person, remember to lift the shorter person up into the air, holding him or her up high enough to have level eye contact with the taller person. Make sure your hands are clean before attempting any introduction that requires lifting.

Dear Jovial Bob:

Is it old-fashioned to call an adult "sir"?

Phoebe
Des Moines, Iowa

No. Even in this day and age, when meeting an adult for the first time, it is still correct to say "sir." Example:

"Blempglorf, may I present Miss Susan Dawson."

"How do you do, sir."

• • • • •

Dear Jovial Bob:

My boyfriend took me to a very crowded, noisy party last Friday night. During the party, I had to introduce some of my friends to some of his friends. Because it was so noisy, I had a really hard time making the introductions. Any suggestions?

Just Wondering
Cleveland, Ohio

At crowded, noisy parties, I recommend memorizing and using the following phrase. These sample introductions will demonstrate its usefulness:

"Rodney, may I present Murrrrgle Murrrrgle."

"Murrrrgle Murrrrgle, this is my friend, Phoebe."

"Murrrrgle Murrrrgle, I'd like you to meet one of my best friends—Murrrrgle Murrrrgle."

Of course the important phrase here is "Murrrrgle Murrrrgle." You should use this phrase to disguise the fact that you have completely forgotten the names of the people you are introducing.

You will find that "Murrrrgle Murrrrgle" is a necessity at just about any party you go to. (Always remember to cover your mouth with your hand when using the phrase, to make it even more unintelligible.)

Don't worry about being discovered. The people you are introducing will *blame themselves* for not listening carefully enough. They will introduce themselves to each other all over again, while you slip quietly over to the snack table and toss three or four dozen of those tiny hotdogs into your mouth.

• • • • •

Dear Jovial Bob:

Whenever I am introduced to someone new, I can never remember his or her name. Any suggestions?

Concerned
Muncie, Indiana

A very simple trick when being introduced to someone new is to try to forget the letters BLEMPGLORF and concentrate on the person's name. Just wipe those letters from your mind. Don't even think about BLEMPGLORF for a second. This should help you remember the person you are meeting for the first time.

• • • • •

Dear Jovial Bob:

What if it doesn't help?

Still Concerned
Still in Muncie, Indiana

Listen carefully. Make sure you hear the person's name correctly. Ask the person who is making the introduction to repeat the name 30 or 40 times until you're sure you've got it.

Then be sure to repeat the name aloud to make certain that you'll remember it. Example:

"Rodney, I'd like you to meet Mr. Brontoglorodoromorotoroflorozorrokorroflorofleer."

"How do you do, Mr. Brontoglorodoromorotoroflorozorrokorroflorofleer. Do you spell your name with one or two a's?"

• shaking hands •

Dear Jovial Bob:

How did the custom of shaking hands get started?

Phoebe
Des Moines, Iowa

The tradition of shaking hands is a very old one. It was begun in 1637 by William Pennsyl (he used to hang around with the Penns). Pennsyl was leader of the first

Pennsylvania Colony. Unfortunately, he accidentally located in Rhode Island.

People in the Pennsylvania Colony greeted each other by shaking feet. But in 1637, Pennsyl noticed that every time people shook feet, they fell over. He decided to solve this problem by asking people in his colony to shake hands instead.

The Pennsylvanians began shaking hands, but unfortunately, they still fell over sometimes. It seems the colony was located on the side of a very steep mountain.

Eventually, all of the people fell right out of the colony. But we've been shaking hands ever since.

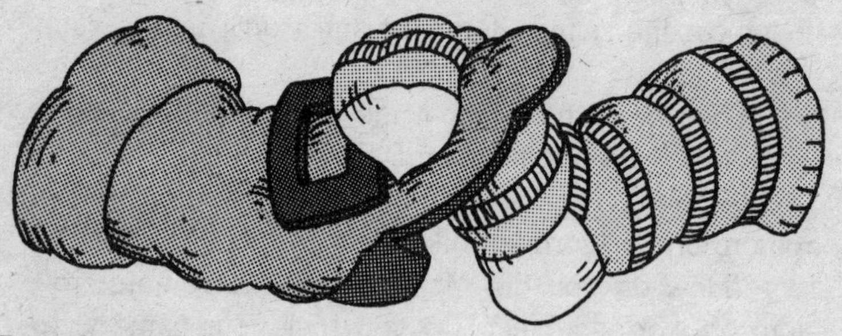

Dear Jovial Bob:

Do you expect me to believe that?

Phoebe
Still in Des Moines, Iowa

• • • • •

Dear Jovial Bob:

When shaking hands with the Queen of England, should one fall to the right knee or the left knee?

Just Wondering
Cleveland, Ohio

It's best to leave the Queen's knees alone!

Dear Jovial Bob:

Is it true that your handshake tells a lot about your personality? Can your handshake really tell people what you are like?

Slick
Boise, Idaho

Dr. Biff Steak, a scientist who takes pictures of people shaking hands when they don't know he's watching, says *yes.* "Handshakes reveal everything about you," says Dr. Steak. "I can even tell by a person's handshake whether that person is a man or a woman—especially if I get a good look at the face!"

What does *your* handshake say about *you?* Here are Dr. Steak's findings:

A WARM, FIRM HANDSHAKE—You are a weak little cowardly runt trying to make up for your pathetic stature with a phony, firm handshake. Shape up—you're not fooling anyone! (fig. 1)

A COLD, LIMP HANDSHAKE—You are strong and confident and don't need to impress people with a firm handshake. (fig. 2)

A COLD, WET HANDSHAKE—It's raining out and you forgot your umbrella. (fig. 3)

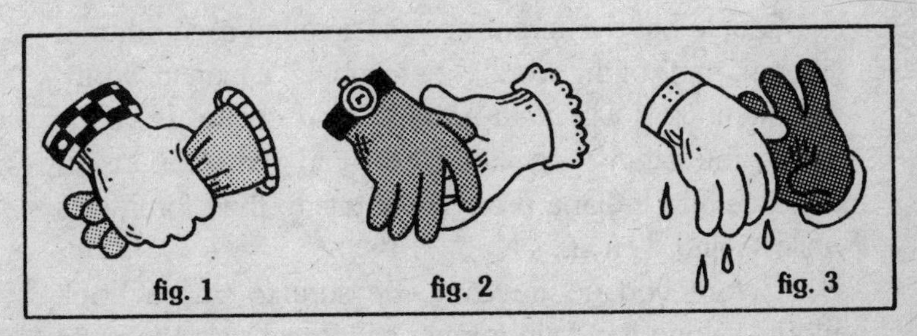

Dear Jovial Bob:

If I can save up enough deposit bottles, I'm going to go on a trip around the world. Before I go, I'd like to clear up one etiquette question. Is shaking hands a proper greeting everywhere? Do people all over the world shake hands?

Traveler
Phoenix, Arizona

NORTHERN BLEMPGLORF

LUWANIA & INDIANA

No. People have different ways of greeting each other in different parts of the world. For example, a man in Northern Blempglorf will greet an old friend on the street by licking the other's necktie. People in remote parts of Luwania and Indiana press wax fruits to their foreheads while saying, "Hiya."

Before you go traveling, be sure to buy a book about shaking hands in foreign countries. I plan to write one as soon as I figure out which hand to write with.

Dear Jovial Bob:

My boyfriend says it's okay to shake hands after a first date. I'm not so sure it's proper. What do you think?

Puzzled
Waco, Texas

I think you need a different book.

• • • • •

Dear Jovial Bob:

Could you repeat everything you've said so far? I started this book in the middle, and I missed the first ten letters or so. Thanks a lot.

Silly Person
Stowe, Vermont

Dear Letter Writers,

Unless I start to get better letters, I'm going to have to end this chapter.

Sincerely,
Jovial Bob

A JOVIAL BOB BONUS GUIDE

(No extra charge for this additional help!)

saying goodbye

It's important to be just as courteous when leaving a room (or being asked to leave a room) as you were when you entered. Be sure to say goodbye with a broad smile and a hearty handshake. As you leave, try not to take items that everyone can plainly see do not belong to you.

Here are three very polite phrases you may wish to memorize. They are sure to be useful at one time or another when saying goodbye.

1. "No hard feelings. I'll be glad to pay for the damages."
2. "Bye now. I hope the swelling goes down real soon."
3. "Okay. All right. I can take a hint. I'm leaving."

JOVIAL BOB'S GOLDEN ETIQUETTE RULE #1

***Please*—not while I'm eating!**

chapter two

dating and going out

According to Dr. Rose E. Complexion of the Bureau of Answers to Most-Often-Asked Questions, the most-often-asked question received in her office is the question of how old is old enough to go out on dates. Quite frankly, she's sick of hearing it!

"Most young people should stay home and read funny etiquette guides instead of going out," says Dr. Complexion, and we couldn't agree with her more.

Here is a short quiz you can take to see if you are ready to go out on dates. Take a look at the following list. Decide which items you would want to take along with you whenever you go out with someone:

1. night light
2. teddy bear
3. security blankie
4. *Old Maid* card game
5. choo choo train
6. baby doll
7. your mother

If you circled one of these items, you are not ready to go out on a date. (A person who is ready will know that it's important to take all *of them along!)*

• • • • •

Dear Jovial Bob:

Perhaps someone has already asked this question, but I'm going to ask it anyway. When is a person old enough to go out on a date?

Hopeful
Twin Forks, Nebraska

Yawn. Let's go on to the next letter.

Dear Jovial Bob:

There's a new girl in my school, and I'd like to ask her out (before she talks to the girls who already know me). My problem is that I don't really know the correct way to ask a girl for a date. Usually I just trip a girl as she walks by and say, "How about it?" But I've had very poor results with that method.

Can you tell me the proper way to ask a girl for a date?

Murray
Miami, Florida

Asking someone for a date isn't really that hard—if you know the correct and polite way to go about it. I'm surprised that the method you've been using hasn't worked. But since it hasn't, here is a list of ways to ask for a date that should bring better results:

1. "Hey—like, know what I mean?"
2. "You don't know me, but would you like to go to Venezuela with me on Saturday?"
3. "I'm willing to give you a break and let you buy me dinner Friday night."
4. "I've tried 16 other people and none of them would go with me to the school dance on Friday. How about you?"
5. "I don't believe you're as dull as everyone says you are. How about a date?"
6. "I'll stop poking you with this stick if you'll go out with me."
7. "If you're not busy on Friday, maybe you'd like to come help me clean the spit valve on my trombone."

Dear Jovial Bob:

On my last date, when I went to pick up Debbie Sue, I stood out on the driveway and yelled, "HONNNNNK! HONNNNNK!" but her parents made me come in anyway. (I guess they knew I wasn't old enough to drive.) Once I got inside, I couldn't think of anything to say to them. Any suggestions?

In A Quandary
Tucson, Arizona

Making conversation with your date's parents is not always easy. Here is a list you might find helpful. It contains five things *not* to say to your date's parents:

1. "What a nice living room. We used to have beat-up old furniture too, and it was very comfortable!"
2. "Gee, I thought you'd be much younger!"
3. "No, please—go right on eating that awful-looking glop. Don't let me interrupt your dinner!"
4. "Don't worry about me keeping her out too late. I'm probably going to ditch her in about ten minutes!"
5. "Could you lend me $10? I'm a little short this week."

• • • • •

Dear Jovial Bob:

Somehow I got roped into taking a date to a formal dinner dance. As you can imagine, I'm hoping to come down with the measles or something. But just in case I don't and I have to go through with this thing, do I have to give the girl flowers?

Unlucky
Pittsburgh, Pennsylvania

Yes, if you are going to a formal dinner dance, it is still the custom for a boy to bring his date flowers. If you pick the flowers yourself, stay away from roses or other flowers with thorns which might cause your date to bleed all over her fancy dress.

Never give a girl a wrist corsage that's bigger than her head. Keep in mind that potted plants are difficult to wear. And remember, flowers that squirt water are almost never in good taste.

Dear Jovial Bob:

Okay, okay, so I'll buy her flowers. But do I have to hold the car door open for her?

Unlucky
Pittsburgh, Pennsylvania

The custom of holding the car door open for one's date actually goes back thousands of years. Today, in some parts of the country, young men who do not have cars still insist on holding car doors for their date.

Girls today don't insist on having doors opened for them, but you may prefer to keep this old custom alive anyway. If you accidentally slam the door on your date's hand and crush her fingers to smithereens, always remember to say, "Excuse me."

• • • • •

Dear Jovial Bob:

Someone told me that when I take a girl out, I should talk to her. Can this be true? Please help me!

Struck Dumb
Cincinnati, Ohio

After several dates you will probably discover that talking is an important part of dating. If you find that it's very quiet in the room and that you're not getting better acquainted at all with your date, it may be because you're not talking.

Making conversation is not difficult if you remember to ask your date questions. Don't try to dominate the conversation by talking about yourself. Show a real interest in your date by trying to find out as much as you can about your date's feelings and ideas. Here are some sample questions you may wish to ask to get the ball rolling:

"What do you think of my hair?"
"How do you like my new shirt?"
"Do you think I have an okay smile?"
"How do you like me so far?"

Compliments will also be appreciated by your date—especially if they are sincere. Here are a few particularly sincere compliments you may wish to memorize and use:

"Gee, your hair is a lot less greasy than usual."

"You're really not as short as you appear to be."

"That new outfit would look great if it fit better."

"I'm only yawning because I feel so comfortable with you."

• • • • •

Dear Jovial Bob:

I'll bet you have even more helpful hints about making small talk, don't you! I'll bet you even have a handy list of four more rules for making successful small talk.

Could you share that list with us?

Rodney
Twin Forks, Nebraska

Yes, as a matter of fact, I could. Here are four additional rules for making successful small talk:

1. Never try to start a conversation when you have a mouth full of raw oysters.

2. Never make small talk when your date's hair is on fire.

3. Never tell your date the same joke more than five times in a single hour.

4. Never begin a conversation with the words, "Now what's wrong with you is. . . ."

Dear Jovial Bob:

I had an upsetting experience last week. Perhaps this has happened to you.

I've been going steady with a girl in my class for about three weeks. Last week I invited her over to meet my parents and stay for dinner. After I introduced her to everyone, she sat down on the couch and said, "I am really starving!" Then she started pulling the fur off my dog and eating it.

What should I do?

Bewildered
Wheeling, West Virginia

Brush your dog vigorously at least twice a day and perhaps no one will notice the bald spots.

Dear Jovial Bob:

Last Friday night my boyfriend invited me to go to a roller disco with him. I looked forward to it all week. But when we got there, he didn't have enough money, and he could only rent one skate.

We had to take turns using the skate, and I was so embarrassed, I just wanted to die! Eventually, the skate broke because I had to put all my weight on it, so we walked home.

I told my date that he's a cheapskate! Do you think I did the right thing?

Phoebe
Des Moines, Iowa

No. I think that's a very bad joke. Please do not write to me again until you have funnier material.

• • • • •

Dear Jovial Bob:

I have some questions about kissing. How do I know if my date wants or expects a good night kiss? Who kisses first, the boy or the girl? How long should a goodnight kiss last?

Rodney
Twin Forks, Nebraska

I'm sorry, Rodney, but I'm saving the answers to those questions for another book. You don't expect me to give away all the fun stuff in just one book, do you?

Keep watching the book stores for my next book, which will be called *The Fun Stuff That Was Left Out Of The Last Book.*

Barney
thank you
for the giant
slab of sheet
metal. you
can imagine
how surprised
was when

chapter three

thank-you notes

Dear Jovial Bob:

I am writing this letter for my daughter, who is too busy writing thank-you notes to write to you. We are having a little disagreement which I hope you can clear up.

Is it necessary for her to send a thank-you note to someone who has given her the correct time? As soon as you give us the answer, I'll make sure that she sends you a thank-you note.

Concerned Parent
Des Moines, Iowa

Dear Jovial Bob:

My mother says I have to send a thank-you note to my friend Donny and thank him because he stopped stepping on my foot. And she says I have to send a thank-you note to Donny's mom for stopping Donny from beating me to a pulp.

Are these notes really necessary? Shouldn't I just sock Donny in the jaw instead?

Ernie
Address Unknown

Dear Jovial Bob:

Please help me! I just wrote a thank-you note to my grandmother for the thank-you note thanking me for the thank-you note I sent after her first thank-you note for my thank-you note.

Isn't there any way to stop this? Or should I just sock Donny in the jaw?

Murray
Miami, Florida

These letters indicate two things to me:

1) Young people are very concerned about thank-you notes.

2) Donny had better lay low for a while.

The truth is, all young people spend at least 80 percent of their time writing thank-you notes. These notes will not be difficult to write if you keep in mind a few simple rules.

The most important rule in thank-you note writing is: Don't be original. All people expect to find certain tried-and-true words and phrases in your thank-you note. Don't disappoint them.

For example, never *write: "It behoovles me to forsofficate my appreciagle for your thogitorious and most glongoremeus present." Even if those are your true feelings, they do not belong in a proper thank-you note.*

Instead, you must use the standard thank-you note phrases and write: "I just had to write and thank you for the lovely blacksmith bellows."

Perhaps the best way to learn how to write thank-you notes correctly is to study some good examples. I don't happen to have any good examples handy, so the following will just have to do.

Dear Grandmother,

Thank you for the book end. I have always admired Bugs Bunny and consider him to be one of our greatest living Americans. So you can imagine how thrilled I was to receive his back and tail on such a beautiful book end.

I know that if I am good this year, you will send me the other book end next year. Then I will have the front of Bugs Bunny, too, and maybe then my books won't keep falling over. That sure is something to look forward to!

Thanks again.

Love,
Stewie

Dear Uncle Barney,

Thank you for the giant slab of sheet metal. You can imagine how surprised I was when my birthday rolled around and you surprised me once again with another slab of that wonderful sheet metal.

I think sheet metal makes a very practical present, and I'd say that even if you weren't in the sheet metal business. My Dad says that someday we'll take the giant slabs of sheet metal you send me every year and cut them down into thousands of small pieces of sheet metal. That will really be exciting!

Thanks again! Your present sure was a surprise!

Yours truly,
Alice

P.S. I'm sorry you weren't able to attend my duckpin juggling recital at school, but thanks anyway for sending over some sheet metal.

Dear Mrs. Blorney,

Thank you for a great weekend at your house. It was so nice of you to invite me. Since Timmy is my best friend at school, I really enjoyed spending time with his whole family.

It was also really nice of you to be such a good sport about those mysterious missing items. I really don't know how all that silverware of yours, Timmy's record albums, and those two Chinese vases ended up in my suitcase. I guess I packed in such a hurry that I accidentally put them in with my stuff.

Mistakes will happen, I guess, but Mom says to tell you you've been very nice about the whole thing. (She hasn't stopped crying or she'd tell you herself.)

Best regards to Mr. Blorney. Hope you'll have me over again real soon.

Sincerely,
Billy

Dear Grandmother,

Mom says to say thank you for the sweater. She says to tell you that it's a beautiful color and has great style.

Dad says to be sure to mention that it's what I've always wanted. Mom says to add that it will go great with my new plaid skirt.

Dad says I should say how nice it was of you to remember me on my birthday.

Mom says to close with

Love,
Polly

• guide to standard thank-you note english •

If those samples do not simplify thank-you note writing for you, this list will certainly do the trick. Here in one handy place are all the phrases you could possibly need for writing thank-you notes. Simply select the phrases you feel are appropriate, put them in the order that seems to make sense to you—and write away! (I'm sure you'll want to send me a thank-you note immediately just for including this helpful list in this helpful book!)

1. I just had to write and thank you for the wonderful whatchamacallit.
2. I can't begin to thank you for your gift, so I won't.
3. I'm sure I will find some use for the wonderful whatchamacallit.
4. I can't begin to thank you since I can't figure out what your present is!
5. You really shouldn't have!
6. It was so nice of you to think of me, even though it was four sizes too small.

7. I was so surprised you remembered—especially since I don't remember you.
8. You really shouldn't have!
9. How did you know I'd been hoping for a 40-pound cheese ball?
10. I never expected that it would bite me back. What a surprise!
11. How did you know that I needed an extra pair of ruffled plaid shirt cuffs?
12. You really shouldn't have!
13. Such an original, unusual present! I really would've been just as happy with cash!
14. All of my friends have wind-up asparaguses—and now, thanks to you, I've got one too!
15. It's just the right size. Mom says I'll grow into it in less than 20 years.
16. It fits perfectly if I roll up newspapers inside it.
17. It's exactly what I would have picked (if I were blind or insane).
18. Pink, fuzzy eyeglass frames go so perfectly with everything I have!
19. You really shouldn't have!
20. Everyone says it's the kind of present only you would buy!
21. You *really* shouldn't have! Really!

JOVIAL BOB'S GOLDEN ETIQUETTE
RULE #2
Go in the other room if you're going to do that!

Dear Moose
Dear Sir
Dear Sir Moose
Dear Mr. Moose
To Moose
It May
Concern:
I have just

chapter four
writing business letters

Dear Jovial Bob:

What are business letters anyway? Why do we send them? What makes a good business letter? How many questions do I have to ask before you get this chapter on business letters started?

Phoebe
Des Moines, Iowa

Dear Jovial Bob:

Can you tell me how to write a proper business letter—*after* I've sealed it in the envelope? Also, what is the proper salutation to use in a business letter to a moose?

Al Antler
Melbourne, Australia

I wish I could answer these very interesting letters in depth, but my dinner is just about ready, so I just can't take the time. Sorry.

There are many ways to communicate with people. At one time, Native Americans used smoke signals to communicate. Today, of course, it's very hard to get smoke signals into envelopes. This is why we send business letters instead.

Because business people are usually extremely busy, it's best to keep a business letter brief and to the point. Always choose an appropriate salutation for your business letter. If you are writing to your Congressman, don't begin, "Dear Sweetyface." If you are writing a letter to your father asking for a bigger allowance in exchange for more responsibilities, and you want to impress him with how mature you are becoming, it's best not to begin your letter, "Dear Da Da."

Here is a business letter written last December by a young man in my neighborhood. He happened to drop it on his way to put it in the mailbox, so I picked it up, opened it, and read it.

There is a very serious mistake in this business letter. Read it carefully and see if you can find it.

Mr. Santa R. Claus
Santa's Workshop
North Pole
Arctic Circle

Dear Mr. Claus:

I hope you're still into the Christmas thing and haven't gone into another business or anything like that. This year, I'd like a Computo-Pet Animal Hospital Set, a Video-Equipped, Life-Sized Slot Car with Track, a Thermal Nuclear Skateboard with Flash Attachment, a pair of socks, a Hydro-Electric Football Game, and a monkey wrench.

I hope you'll remember the less-fortunate kids in my neighborhood, too— after you remember me.

If you do not bring me the items I've asked for so politely, I will politely punch your face until it looks like a cabbage that's been through a blender.

Yours truly,
Tad Pole

Did you find the mistake in this letter? That's right— Tad forgot to include Santa's zip code. Always include the zip code on all your business correspondence.

• two examples •

Business letters should state clearly what you have in mind. They should also give the person receiving the letter a good reason to read it. For example, here is an example of a poorly written business letter:

poor example

Mr. Wadsworth Fenn
Circulation Department
Muncie Courier & Post-Dispatch Journal Enquirer Express Star World Tribune & Examiner
11114 Easy Street
Muncie, Indiana

Dear Mr. Fenn:

I am applying for the job of newspaper delivery boy. I would like this job because I am hoping to save enough money to go to college and study journalism.

I know I could do a good job. I have helped my brother deliver the Courier & Post-Dispatch Journal Enquirer Express Star World Tribune & Examiner for the past three years.

If there is an opening, I would be glad to come down to your office to discuss the job with you. I look forward to hearing from you.

Yours truly,
Ty Shulaces
Ty Shulaces

Ty's letter follows the proper form for a business letter, but he doesn't give Mr. Fenn any reason to read his letter. Now, compare Ty's poor letter to this excellent example of a business letter. . . .

excellent example

Mr. Wadsworth Fenn
Circulation Department
Muncie Courier & Post-Dispatch Journal Enquirer
Express Star World Tribune & Examiner
1114 Easy Street
Muncie, Indiana

Dear Mr. Fenn,

I am applying for the job of newspaper delivery boy. I would like this job because I understand the tips are pretty good, and you get to read the funnies before anyone else. I know I could do a good job because I really like to throw things, and I'm always riding my bike over people's lawns anyway.

MY DADS cousin is married to the owner of your newspaper, and when they were over for supper the other night, he said SURE, I could have a job with the paper, or he'd know the reason why. I hope you'll consider me for the job.

Yours truly,
Ted E. Bear

Now, if you were Mr. Fenn, which young man would *you* give the job to?

Of course Ted got the job—at a starting salary of $10,000 a year—all because he knew how to write a proper business letter.

chapter five

for boys: how to dress correctly

Dear Jovial Bob:

My parents say that since I'm old enough to write letters to you, I'm old enough to own my first suit. Could you give me some advice on the best way to go about buying a suit?

Rodney
Twin Forks, Nebraska

The best place to buy a suit is a clothing shop or department store. Stay away from stores that sell both men's suits and live bait. Also, stay away from clothing stores that are located in illegally parked trailers.

Take your time when buying a suit. Don't allow a fast-talking salesperson to persuade you to make an impractical purchase. Sure, that sheepskin suit will keep you warm all winter. But unless you work after school as a shepherd, it probably isn't in style in your neighborhood.

Never listen to a salesperson who attempts to sell you a short-sleeved suit for summer wear, or a sponge suit to wear underwater.

Be careful not to spend too much—or too little—for your suit. One hundred dollars is a bit steep for a three-piece suit (with vest) made of construction paper. And think twice about a custom made, gray wool suit with two pairs of trousers that is being offered to you for 49¢ and one bottle top.

Another hint: Stay away from cereal boxes that advertise "Free Sports Jacket Inside!" The jackets almost never fit properly, and it's impossible to get the cornflakes out of the pockets.

HOW TO INSPECT THE SUIT

Always check the workmanship of a suit you are thinking of buying. Check for the following:

THE STITCHING

Is the suit stitched together with thread or thin spaghetti? Is it stapled together? Is the collar stitched up so tight your head won't fit through? Are the sleeves stitched to the rest of the jacket, or do they come separately?

THE LINING

Is the pattern of the lining correct? (You don't want a checked lining inside a polka dot suit.) Is the lining made of good material, or is it made of lint? Is the lining on the inside or the outside of the jacket?

THE BUTTON HOLES

Are the button holes on the front or back of the jacket? Are the button holes larger than your fist? Do the button holes fall off if you shake the jacket?

THE POCKETS

Do the pockets open from the top or bottom? Are there wet, sticky things inside the pockets?

Next, check to see if the suit fabric wrinkles. You don't want to buy a suit that wrinkles easily. Take the suit off the hanger and roll it up into a tiny ball. Drop it onto the floor and pour a bucket of water over it. Jump up and down on the suit. Now run in place on top of the suit for about ten minutes.

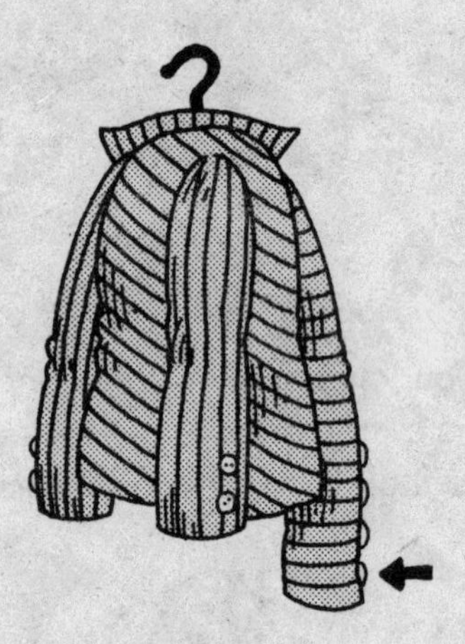

Pick up the suit and unroll it. Is it at all wrinkled? If so, ask to see another suit.

Finally, try on the suit and check the fit. Inspect to see where each sleeve falls. The first jacket sleeve should end about half an inch from your shirt cuff. The second sleeve should also end about half an inch from the shirt cuff. If the third sleeve is not exactly the same length as the first two, do not buy the suit.

how to tie a tie

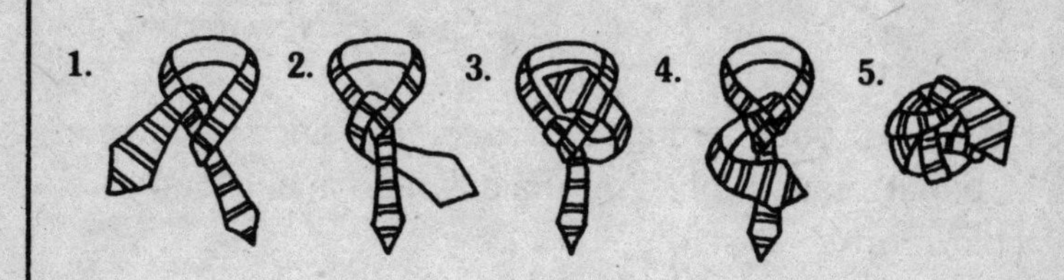

INCORRECT

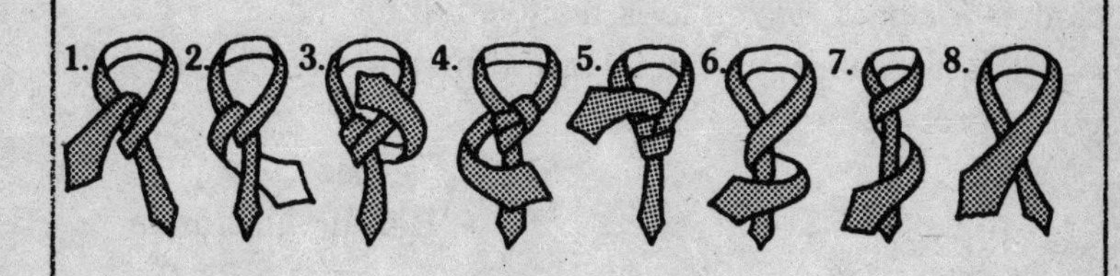

INCORRECT

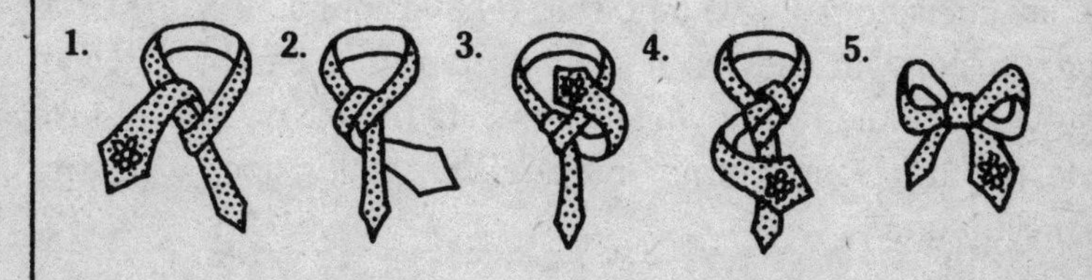

CORRECT

Dear Jovial Bob:

I have bright orange skin, so I always buy bright orange clothes to match it. I'm very lonely. What am I doing wrong?

Bright Orange Person
Orange, New Jersey

I love your bright orange stationery, but since you wrote in bright orange ink, I'm afraid I can't make out your letter. Sorry.

• • • • •

Dear Jovial Bob:

I have wavy blond hair, piercing blue eyes, handsomely tanned skin, and my parents buy me all the latest designer clothes for boys, which look really great on me.

I don't have a question. I just wanted to describe myself in your book.

Terrific Guy
Bel Air, California

• • • • •

Dear Jovial Bob:

Is it okay to wear pink and yellow plaid slacks with a gray, green, and blue pull-over shirt? Is it okay to wear blue and white checked pants with no shirt (I have light pink skin)? Does brown go with red? Is it ever proper to wear brown with brown? Should I wear white with white (or will people mistake me for the Good Humor man)? What color goes well with sea-slug gray?

Rodney
Twin Forks, Nebraska

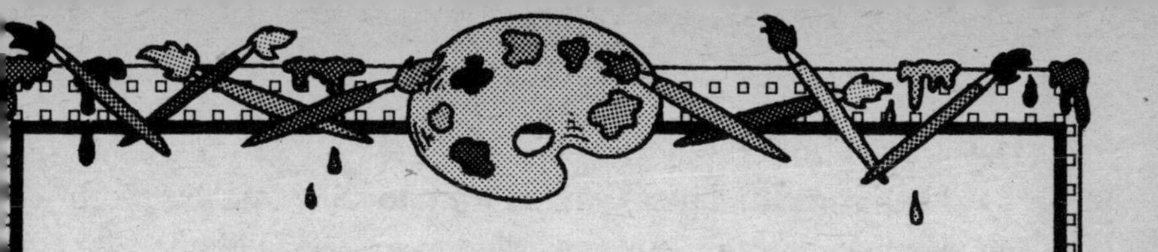

WHAT COLORS SHOULD YOU WEAR?

Now that you have purchased a suit, you'll need to coordinate the rest of your clothing to present a fashionably correct appearance.

In order to know what colors you should wear with what, it is important to study color theory and philosophy, light coordination, and the metaphysics of light refraction. Until you have time to complete these studies, you may use the following chart:

IF YOUR HAIR IS BROWN:
Always wear grays, tans, greens, and blues.
IF YOUR HAIR IS BLACK:
Always wear grays, tans, greens, and blues.
IF YOUR HAIR IS RED:
Always wear greens, blues, grays, and tans.
IF YOUR HAIR IS BLONDE:
Always wear blues, greens, tans, and grays.
IF YOUR SKIN IS LIGHT:
Avoid blues, greens, tans, and grays.
IF YOUR SKIN IS DARK:
Avoid dark blues, dark greens, dark tans, and dark grays.
IF YOUR SKIN IS BLUE:
See your doctor immediately!

Dear Jovial Bob:

I had some bad news when I went to my closet this morning. My best dress-up suit is starting to lose its feathers. What should I do?

Depressed
Holyoke, Massachusetts

That's funny. I have the same problem with mine! Not only that, but my suit tried to fly south for the winter!

• • • • •

Dear Jovial Bob:

What color tie should I wear with a bearskin suit?

Rodney
Twin Forks, Nebraska

Wear a turtleneck vest and you won't need a tie.

Dear Jovial Bob:

All the kids in my school wear tutus and tights. I feel really out of it in my bluejeans and t-shirts. What should I do?

Murray
Miami, Florida

You have accidentally enrolled in a ballet school. Transfer immediately so your wardrobe will not be out of place.

Dear Jovial Bob:

I recently took up jogging. To be in style, I bought a very fancy running suit, the top line running shoes, and other equipment necessary to participate in this sport, such as running tweezers and ankle brushes.

The total bill came to $850. How should I present this bill to my parents? Do you think they'll understand that this is a real necessity?

Jogger
Bear Run, Missouri

I'd make sure your legs are in good shape for running *before* you present them with the bill.

Dear Jovial Bob:

I think it's really macho for a guy to wear a lot of gold and silver chains around his neck and to keep his shirt unbuttoned down to the waist. My only problem is that 10 or 12 of the chains I'm wearing seem to have gotten caught under my chair leg, so if I stand up, I'll strangle myself.

Any suggestions?

Macho Man
Chicago, Illinois

No. Not at the moment.

Dear Jovial Bob:

My parents ran away from home when I was born, and I have been brought up by my grandmother. She is a very nice woman, but she doesn't know about new clothing styles.

All of the clothes she buys me seem to be from another century. My shirts all have collars that come off. The other kids wear t-shirts to school, and I have to wear a three-piece suit with a waistcoast and spats. My grandmother also makes me wear a derby hat.

Recently, I've gotten very interested in a girl in my class. Every time I go up to talk to her, though, she just looks annoyed and walks away.

Any suggestions?

Unfashionable
Delaware, Maryland

The girl may be annoyed at you because of your lack of manners. You should always tip your derby when in the presence of a lady.

Dear Jovial Bob:

I go to a very fancy school with a lot of kids who are much richer than I am. They wear better clothes than I do, and I think this is causing me to be an outsider. They look down on me because of my less expensive clothes and because I can't dress as nicely as they do.

Recently, I have taken to stealing their clothes and wearing them around school. This has worked out very well. I'm starting to get some new friends because I am wearing better clothes. In fact, I am wearing some of my new friends' clothes (but they don't realize this)!

My problem is that I have been invited to one of my new friend's fancy homes for a yachting weekend. I've never been on a yachting weekend, and I don't know what kind of clothing to steal so that I will be dressed appropriately.

Can you help me?

Teen Thief
Shelton, Connecticut

I'd recommend that you steal both light-weight and warm-weather outfits since the weather can sometimes be unpredictable. A pair of white trousers for afternoon wear would be suitable, as well as a few sweaters of varying weight. Steal a few striped t-shirts in case it gets really warm during the day.

Do any of your friends wear an adult size 36?

Dear Jovial Bob:

Me and some of the guys I hang around with were invited to a party on the planet Muckle. We were told that the party was come-as-you-are, so we just wore our regular school clothes.

But when we arrived on the planet, we noticed that the hosts were wearing greezles, blem, and full griggle on their freels. Some of the other guests were wearing their best dreezles, including glormets, flarn, blempglorf, and froggles in their lapels.

My question is, do you think we offended our hosts by wearing jeans and t-shirts? We were eager to make a good impression—especially since the Muckles have been known to eat humans if annoyed.

Just Wondering
Twin Forks, Nebraska

Of *course* jeans and t-shirts were appropriate—as long as you also wore full friggles on your gremble!

chapter six

for girls: how to dress correctly

Dear Jovial Bob:

Everyone in my school is always worrying about what to wear and what not to wear, and I think it's a lot of baloney! What difference does it make anyway? I don't mean to be rude—but who cares?

Phoebe
Des Moines, Iowa

Dear Jovial Bob:

I am 12 and I'm a little insecure about buying my clothes for the first time. How do I know if the clothes I select fit or not?

Can you give me some tips?

A Little Insecure
Newark, New Jersey

Before you purchase any article of clothing, be sure to try it on in the store. If you cannot squeeze your head through the neck of a sweater, this is a small hint that the sweater might not fit. If you find that, to walk properly, you must fill up your shoes with the rolled-up Sunday newspapers, the shoes may be the wrong size. If the jeans you have selected are so tight you can barely walk or breathe in them, they fit correctly.

CORRECT INCORRECT

Dear Jovial Bob:

My parents always say that it's not polite to go out in public if you're not looking your best. I agree with them, but I have a very small wardrobe, so it's often hard to look my best.

Should I just spend the rest of my life in my room writing letters to silly books like yours—or do you have some tips on how to take care of the clothing I own?

Nervous Young Lady
Newark, New Jersey

Your parents are right. When people meet you for the first time, the second thing they notice about you is the way your clothes look. (The *first* thing they notice is that green stuff stuck to your front teeth from lunch. What are you going to do about *that?*)

To give the right impression, you want to be dressed neatly, whether you own closets filled with clothes or just one dress and one sock. Here are seven tips for taking care of your wardrobe:

1. You don't have to remove your pockets to clean them.
2. Never iron suede shoes.
3. Use a hanger to hang up your shirts—not a meat hook.
4. Don't allow your clothes to pile up on the floor where they may get stepped on. Instead, let them pile up on a chair or under the bed.
5. Fold your sweaters and skirts neatly before throwing them into a corner.
6. Rolling your clothes up into a tight ball will save valuable dresser drawer space.
7. To make sure you don't lose any buttons, remove them from your blouses each night before you go to sleep.

• • • • •

Dear Jovial Bob:

I am 13 and I want to wear lipstick. But my mother says I am only old enough to wear it on one lip. She says girls shouldn't wear it on both lips until they are at least 17 and four months. I think I should be allowed to wear it on both lips since all the other girls in my class do. Who is right?

My mother says that if you take my side, she'll come over there and club you about the head until you scream for mercy. But I know you won't let that stand in the way of your giving the correct advice.

One Lip
Newark, New Jersey

Your mother is definitely right.

• • • • •

Dear Jovial Bob:

When I came home with the outfit I had bought for the first day of school, my mother threw a fit. She yelled and screamed and threw my father out the window—all because she said the outfit I picked out was inappropriate. She said it was in atrocious taste and not right for school.

I think she's off her nut, but I'll let you decide. Here's what I bought:

A green, gold, gray, and maroon tank top; orange designer jeans with cobalt blue pockets; blue, red, and yellow running shoes; and a red V-necked sweatshirt that says "HELLO" in silver sequins on the front and "SORRY I MISSED YOU" in gold sequins on the back.

Well? What do you think? Is the outfit inappropriate for the first day of school?

Fashion Conscious
Newark, New Jersey

No, it's not inappropriate. But why don't you choose an outfit that's a little more unusual? Why do you want to look exactly like every other girl in your class?

Dear Jovial Bob:

I try to be in style and keep up with what the kids are wearing, but I seem to have very sensitive skin. The new blouse I bought itches so badly that I have to stay home and scratch all day.

Any suggestions for me?

Worried Sick
Newark, New Jersey

Perhaps you have selected a fabric that is too coarse for you. Stay away from such fabrics as steel wool, barbed wire, and cut glass with steel carpet tacks embroidered in.

Most girls today lean toward cotton, linen, or silk. I don't know why they're leaning. Perhaps their blouses are tucked in too far.

Dear Jovial Bob:

If I have to go to a party, or to school, or to a friend's house, I always have trouble deciding what is just right to wear.

Could you help me out? You haven't helped anyone else in this chapter, but there's always a first time!

Phoebe
Des Moines, Iowa

Here is a basic guide to the proper attire for each of your day-to-day activities. If you don't wish to wear attire, you may substitute clothing.

FOR SCHOOL:
jeans/blouse/sweaters in matching or contrasting colors

FOR AROUND HOME:
jeans/blouse/sweaters in matching or contrasting colors

FOR VISITING RELATIVES OR FRIENDS:
jeans/blouse/sweaters in matching or contrasting colors

FOR PARTIES:
good jeans/good blouse/good sweaters in matching or contrasting colors

Dear Jovial Bob:

I have a friend who's always putting me down for the color combinations I choose to wear. When I decided to wear a green top with a blue skirt, she told me, "Don't wear the green with the blue."

I was so upset, I went home and changed.

Before the spring dance, I picked out a pink top and a red skirt. She came over just before my date came to pick me up and said, "Don't wear the pink with the red."

I was so upset, I stayed home that night.

She's always butting in. For my date next weekend, I've picked out a black top and a brown skirt. I just know she's going to come over and put her two cents in.

What should I do?

Fit To Be Tied
Newark, New Jersey

Don't wear the black with the brown.

Dear Jovial Bob:

I wrote to you earlier in this chapter because my mother would only let me wear lipstick on one lip. Now I'm writing to you because of earrings.

My mother won't let me wear earrings to the rock concert I'm going to on Friday. She says that vibrations from loud music will cause the earrings to melt and then stick to my ears for the rest of my life.

I don't think that loud rock music can melt earrings—especially the plastic ones I own. Who is right? My mother or me?

My mother says that if you take my side this time, she'll come over there and squeeze your head until it looks like a grape. But I know that you won't let that stand in the way of your giving the correct advice.

One Lip And No Earrings
Newark, New Jersey

Your mother is right again! Aren't you lucky to have such a wise and knowledgeable mother!

JOVIAL BOB'S GOLDEN ETIQUETTE
RULE #3
Leave that disgusting thing outside where it belongs!

chapter seven

parties and dances

• parties •

Dear Jovial Bob:

I am 12 and I am giving my first boy-girl party. I'm selecting the food, the music, the activities—everything—and I'm a little nervous about it.

Can you give me some tips on how to prepare for this party?

Cindy
Newark, New Jersey

First of all, don't be nervous. If your party is a flop, what's the worst thing that could happen? Probably no one will ever speak to you again, you'll lose all your friends, and you'll be a laughingstock in school. Is that anything to be nervous about?

The secret to a good party is to plan carefully in advance. With the right planning, your friends will not only enjoy the party, but they'll do less than $1,000 damage to your house.

Dear Jovial Bob:

That last bit of advice wasn't helpful at all, and now I'm more nervous than ever. Do you think you could be a bit more specific? What kinds of plans should I be making?

Please answer. I'm shaking like a leaf.

Cindy
Newark, New Jersey

First of all, give careful thought to the furniture arrangement. I've found that young people tend to ruin furniture at parties. To avoid this problem, simply remove all the furniture from your house.

One way in which young people tend to ruin furniture is by smearing food on it. Food can be extremely messy—especially if people try to eat it—and I've seen it completely destroy more than one party. So in making your plans, be sure not to plan on serving any food.

Nothing gets the neighbors more angry and upset than loud music coming from a young person's party. So be careful not to play any music at your party.

What could be more boring than a lot of silly party games that people feel foolish participating in? Don't let the absurd games that people usually play at parties ruin your party. Be careful not to plan on any games.

If you remove all the furniture, don't serve food, don't play music, and don't have any games, your party is bound to be a huge success—thanks to careful planning.

• • • • •

Dear Jovial Bob:

I've decided not to give a party after all. I think I'd rather stay in my room and do my geography homework. It sounds like a lot more fun.

Unfortunately, I've already sent out the invitations. Is there a polite way to tell my friends not to come?

Cindy
Newark, New Jersey

No, I don't think there is. But I'm glad you've decided to cancel your party. From the plans you were making, it sounded really dullsville.

• • • • •

Dear Jovial Bob:

I don't have a question about parties, but it's been pages and pages since I had a letter in your book, so I just thought I'd write and say hi.

Rodney
Twin Forks, Nebraska

Dear Jovial Bob:

My teenage son is giving a party for several boys and girls in his class. He says that modern parents don't hang around these days when their kids give a party, and he has asked my husband and myself to go stay in another city on the night of the party.

Is this right? Some of his friends are a bit rowdy. (Many of them have prison records.) What should I do?

Concerned Parent
Cincinnati, Ohio

Explain to your son that you really do trust and respect him, but you think that just a little supervision might be a good idea. Then be sure to have at least one adult chaperone on hand for each friend he invites.

• dances •

Dear Jovial Bob:

I've been invited to a formal dinner-dance. My date for the evening is an 800-pound elk. Should I buy him flowers even though I know he'll just eat them as soon as he gets them?

Millie
South Bend, Indiana

I think the authorities should send someone to South Bend to see what's going on out there!

• • • • •

Dear Jovial Bob:

All right, so I'm not such a hot dancer. All that disco music hurts my head and I get a little confused. So, all right, I stepped on my date's feet a few times, and her left foot swelled up so big we couldn't get it through the door.

So, all right, I accidentally kicked her a few times and now she can't go out for cheerleading because she has bruises all over her leg. All right. So I was doing the Bump and accidentally threw her hip out of joint and she had to be put in traction for a few weeks.

I admit I'm not such a hot dancer.

But is that any reason for her to call me a "stupid, bumbling, idiotic, imbecilic, clumsy ox"? I think she was being very rude. Don't you agree?

Wounded Pride
Houston, Texas

Yes, I do agree. I don't think it was polite of her to say that you were bumbling.

• • • • •

Dear Jovial Bob:

I am 13 and I went with a boy I know to a dance at school last Friday night. He picked me up at 7:30 and his father drove us to the dance.

Then he spent the entire time ignoring me. He stayed with all the boys on one side of the gym, and all the girls were on the other side. He never danced with me once. All he did was laugh with his friends, throw food, shove other guys, and get into fights.

His father picked us up at 11:30 and took me home. The boy thanked me for a great evening.

Is this normal?

Becky Sue Lynne Jeannie May
Atlanta, Georgia

No, it isn't. Boys usually aren't that polite.

AN EASY DANCE STEP FOR YOU TO LEARN

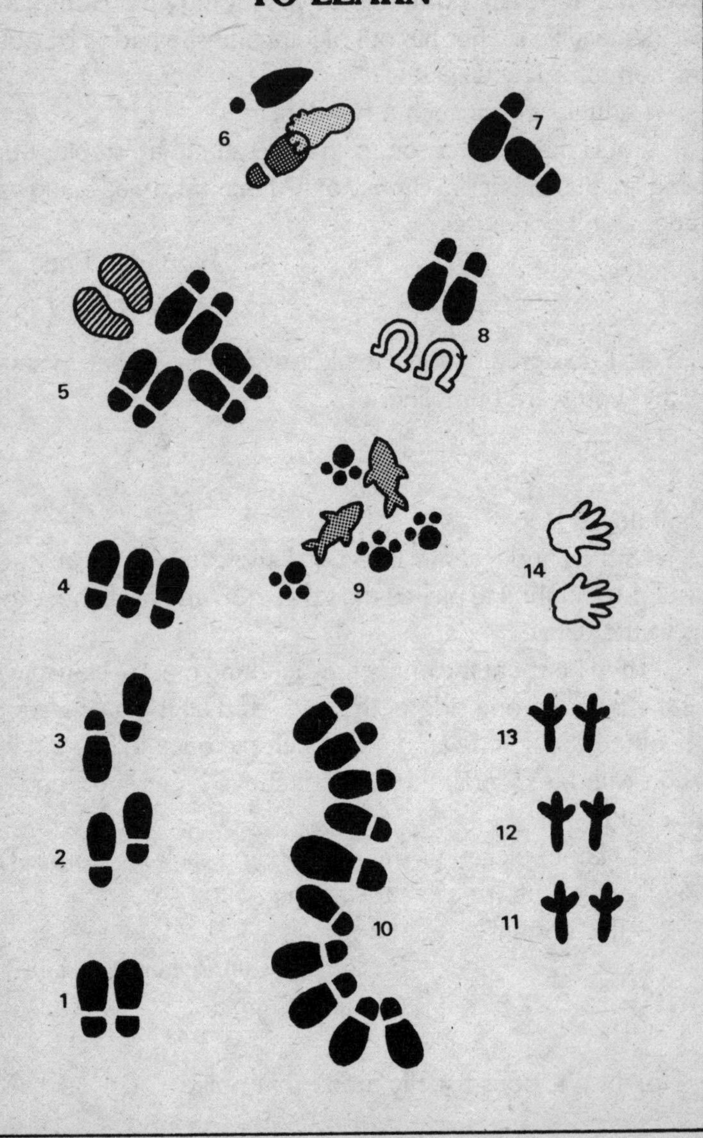

A JOVIAL BOB BONUS QUESTION

(No extra charge for this additional help! Well . . . maybe just a few cents more.)

Dear Jovial Bob:

I've become very friendly with a talking horse. I have long discussions about all kinds of subjects with him. I really feel that this horse is the only one in the world who truly understands me.

On the night of the big football game, my parents' car broke down. I desperately needed a ride to the game. My father said, "Why don't you ride the horse to the game?"

But the horse is my best friend.

Wouldn't it be rude to ride my best friend to a football game? And do you think I'm crazy for spending so much time talking to a horse?

Puzzled
Frankfort, Kentucky

I discussed your question at length with a duck that wanders into my back yard from time to time, and we both decided that you're nuts!

chapter eight

table manners

Dear Jovial Bob:

When I eat, I like to really throw myself into it. I usually end up with tomato sauce smeared all over my face and body, noodles dripping from my hair, and pieces of meat in my pockets and all over the floor.

Do you have any suggestions for me?

Big Eater
Palm Beach, Florida

Yes. Remind me never to invite you over for dinner.

• • • • •

Dear Jovial Bob:

What is the proper way to lick gravy off a dinner plate? From right to left, or left to right?

Polite Person
Walnut Creek, California

I'm sorry. I cannot answer your question. You have not told me whether you are licking the gravy off your own plate or the plate of the person next to you.

Dear Jovial Bob:

Should clam shells be cracked with a hammer or smashed with a baseball bat?

Shell Shocked
Muncie, Indiana

Yes.

• • • • •

Dear Jovial Bob:

I think silverware is a wonderful invention, and I try to use it whenever possible. Who invented silverware anyway?

Silverware Freak
Salt Lake City, Utah

Silverware was invented by an anonymous caveman named Hy O'Silver in 1965. (To this day, no one knows why O'Silver was still living in a cave in 1965!)

He was attempting to invent the radio, but he came up with silverware instead. Unfortunately, he wasted 12 years trying to get music from his fork!

• • • • •

Dear Jovial Bob:

Speaking of forks, can you tell me what one is?

Rodney
Twin Forks, Nebraska

This question is much too babyish to be answered here. You'd have to be born on Mars not to know what a fork is!

Dear Jovial Bob:

I was born on Mars. Can you tell me what a fork is?

Oxni Gleckle IV
Columbus, Ohio

Come on, gang—isn't anyone taking this book seriously?!?

• • • • •

Dear Jovial Bob:

When should I use a fork?

Rodney's Little Brother
Twin Forks, Nebraska

I'm getting more than a little fed up with these silly fork questions. Now unless someone has something more interesting to ask, I'm going to close this chapter and go take a nap!

• • • • •

Dear Jovial Bob:

Should I use a fork to pick up my spoon?

Unsigned
Twin Forks, Nebraska

THAT DOES IT!! I don't like to lose my temper in a book—especially a book about manners—but I'VE HAD IT!! HAD IT!! DO YOU HEAR ME? No more fork questions!! *Please!* How about a good question about punch bowls? You must have something you need to know about punch bowls! Come on, how about it? Punch bowls, anyone?

Dear Jovial Bob:

I dropped my fork into the punch bowl. What's my question?

Phoebe
Des Moines, Iowa

Okay. All right. You win.

I guess you think you've put one over on Jovial Bob. Well, I do have ways of getting back at you, you know. How would you like a 30-page discussion on How To Fold A Napkin Properly? You wouldn't—would you! So shape up!

Dear Jovial Bob:

I have a question for you that has been on my mind for several years. Can you tell me how to fold a napkin properly? Is there any way I can get it to stay under my chin without using staples?

Eddie
Somewhere in the Desert

Now here—at last—is an intelligent question! Unfortunately, there's no intelligent answer for it, so we'd better go on to the next one. Sorry, Eddie. Hope those staples aren't too painful!

Dear Jovial Bob:

Every time I try to eat corn flakes with a fork, the corn flakes go up my nose instead of into my mouth. Sometimes I end up with an entire bowl of corn flakes up my nose.

What should I do about this?

Beside Myself
Ogden, Utah

Don't worry—that happens to everyone.

• • • • •

Dear Jovial Bob:

Is it proper to eat chicken with your hands?

Rodney
Twin Forks, Nebraska

Yes—but always wait until the bird has been killed and plucked before picking it up to eat it.

• • • • •

Dear Jovial Bob:

Is there a right way and a wrong way to set the table? I'll bet there is—and I'll bet you're dying to tell us about it.

Phoebe
Des Moines, Iowa

There *is* a right way and a wrong way to set the table. A table that is set the wrong way can cause confusion to guests, violent arguments, and unnecessary fork wounds.

To avoid such problems, familiarize yourself with every piece of silverware and crockery in your house. Run your hands over each piece until you can tell by touch the difference between a potato wrench and a grape tweezer, between an avocado plunger and a hamburger chisel, between a bread fork and a left-handed egg sucker.

SETTING FOR AN INFORMAL DINNER

Incorrect

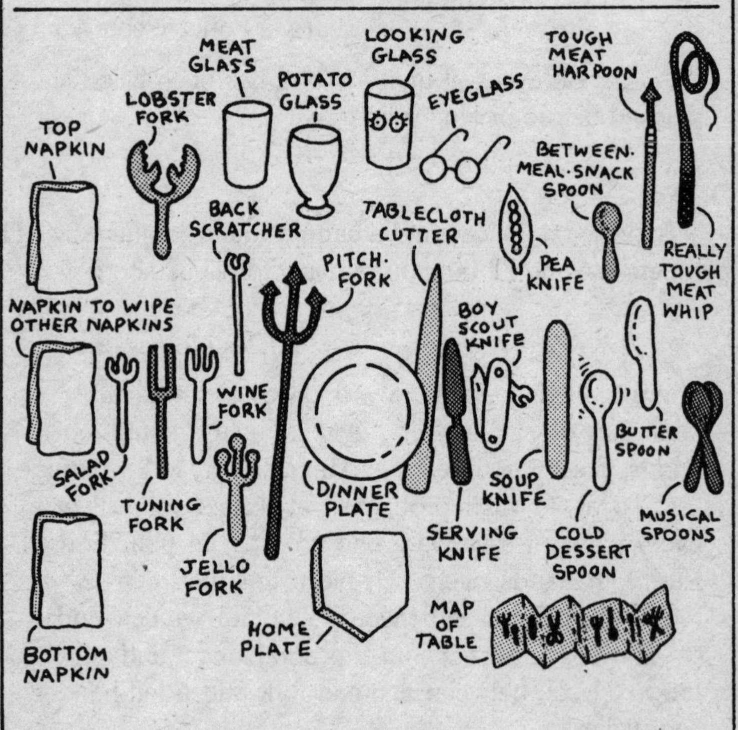

Correct

Dear Jovial Bob:

My aunt took me to a fancy restaurant where I tried a lot of interesting dishes for the first time. After dinner, I ordered a flaming dessert, and I must say I found it very disappointing.

In fact, when I started to eat it, I got third degree burns all over my face and had to be hosed down with a sprinkler. Any suggestions?

Burnt Gourmet
Salem, Massachusetts

That's funny. The same thing happened to me last week! Someone told me it might have been a good idea to wait for the flames to go out *before* I started to slurp the dessert from the bowl.

Dear Jovial Bob:

I have been invited to a formal dress, sit-down breakfast, and I'm a little nervous about it. Perhaps you can help me. Should I drink my orange juice from my right hand or my left hand? And which side should I butter my toast on?

Timid Eater
Atlanta, Georgia

You should drink your orange juice from a glass—not from your hand. And you should butter your toast on the outside.

CORRECT INCORRECT

Dear Jovial Bob:

Whenever dinner time rolls around, I have this uncontrollable urge to get up from my chair, climb up onto the table, and sit down in my dinner plate. Whenever I do this, I am severely criticized by my family and friends.

Are they right for saying that I am being impolite?

Out of Control
Dayton, Ohio

Yes, your family and friends are right when they criticize you. It is extremely rude to climb up on the table and sit in your dinner plate. Always bring the plate down to your chair when you wish to sit in it.

Dear Jovial Bob:

My house is on a hill, so the peas always roll off my plate. What can I do?

Topsy Turvy
South Bend, Indiana

About what?

Dear Jovial Bob:

I know you're anxious to finish this chapter so you can go out and water your moat. But before you do, do you think you could give us five more tips for good table manners?

Desperate
Twin Forks, Nebraska

Yes, I'd be delighted to. (Such a polite letter!) Here are five etiquette tips which I've always found to come in handy wherever I go:

1. Never wipe your mouth with your shirt cuff—unless you have already used the back of your hand.
2. Never squeeze hamsters at the dinner table unless dessert has already been served.
3. Never show off by carrying a whole roast turkey to the dinner table in your teeth.
4. A dead bird should always be passed from left to right until everyone has had a chance to see it at least once.
5. When leaving the table, it's impolite to take the tablecloth with you.

A JOVIAL BOB BONUS GUIDE!

21 ADDITIONAL RULES OF ETIQUETTE YOU SHOULD MEMORIZE IMMEDIATELY

1. Young women should not chew tobacco when curtseying to the Queen of England.
2. It's not polite to eat pork and beans with your fingers without offering a handful to your date.
3. People who set fire to the drapes are seldom invited back.
4. Never throw lima beans at someone who is expecting peas.
5. It's rude to warm your hands on the head of a bald person unless it's very cold out.
6. Raw meat should not be worn to Presidential inaugurations.
7. At birthday parties, it's usually considered rude to sit on the cake before six p.m.
8. When meeting someone for the first time, placing four fingers in your nose will probably not make a good impression.
9. Never slap a friend during a tornado.

10. Girls who wear oleomargarine in their ears will not be asked out a second time.
11. It is considered rude to put the phone receiver in your mouth and make sucking noises while speaking long distance.
12. It's bad manners to bring a violently ill chimpanzee to a formal wedding.
13. Always use a salad fork to pick up any ants you kill at the dinner table.
14. Never eat anything that speaks three languages.
15. It's considered rude to sit in the lap of a person who is having dental surgery.
16. Always say "Pardon me" after backing a car over someone who is well dressed.
17. When staying overnight at a friend's house, do not drink the aquarium.
18. It's considered bad manners to lend your father's best pair of slacks to a horse.
19. On a picnic, the picnic basket should not be eaten until all the sandwiches are gone.
20. Always use a long-handled spoon to remove raw hamburger from your shirt pocket.
21. Don't stand in the soup.

IMPORTANT BONUS LETTER

Dear Jovial Bob,

Im terribly sorry but
Ive compleatly forgotten
what I wanted to write
to you about. It slipped
~~rite~~ right out of my
mind. How silly of me!

Forgetful Phil
Bronx, New York

• contributors •

Although Jovial Bob has told everyone he knows that he wrote this book himself, the truth is that no book as complicated, as complete, and as totally useless as this one could have been written alone. The contributors to this book insisted again and again (and even pleaded) that their names not be mentioned. But we feel strongly that they are entitled to what is coming to them, and so here are the experts who must share responsibility for this book:

DR. MENDEL CASE

Dr. Case is the world expert on when it is polite to stand up and when it is polite to sit down. For the past 44 years, he has been following people, watching them carefully, and taking pictures of them standing up and sitting down. Dr. Case plans to continue his studies even though most people wish he would just go away.

DR. BYRD BRANE

Dr. Brane has spent the past 22 years following Dr. Mendel Case. Night and day, Dr. Brane has taken pictures of Dr. Case standing up, sitting down, and then standing up again—and quite frankly, he's getting a little dizzy!

DOTTY S.A. FRUTECAKE

Ms. Frutecake is the well-known author of *It Isn't Polite To Point,* the first manners book for dogs. Next fall, her second book, *Pardon My Beak,* a manners guide for African Gray Parrots, will be published, and it will probably be laughed at, too.

HARDY BREAKFAST

Hardy has been experimenting with sponges for several years. No one is really sure why.

CLEMMA CHOWDER

Although she was never fortunate enough to be a teenager herself, Ms. Chowder always dreamed of helping either teenagers or gorillas born in captivity. Last spring, police shut down her etiquette academy and used-bait-shop and threw away the key.

ROMAINE LETTUCE, JR.

Since he began his underwater study of the table manners of the common sea slug, Mr. Lettuce has not surfaced even once. We hope he's all right.

ABOUT JOVIAL BOB STINE

Little is known about the real Jovial Bob Stine, and even less is known about his second cousin. (For example: Does he *have* a second cousin?)

People who claim to know Jovial Bob say that they don't know him at all. To others, the name sounds quite a bit like a kind of purple fungus that cannot grow under any conditions.

How he came to write this etiquette guide for young people is an even bigger mystery. According to his second cousin, we don't know the half of it.

We *do* know that thousands of letters from young people began to arrive unexpectedly at Jovial Bob's house. Many of these letters were sticky and disgusting. Some of them contained bits of salami and slices of spicy knockwurst. All of the letters asked for advice.

These young people had etiquette questions that needed to be answered.

Jovial Bob was confused. He couldn't decide whether to use the letters to write an etiquette book—or to feed the letters to his cat.

Luckily for everyone, he did both.

ABOUT CAROL NICKLAUS